First published in Great Britain in 1999 by Bloomsbury Publishing Plc
38 Soho Square, London W1V 5DF

Fran's Flower
Text copyright © 1999 by Lisa Bruce
Illustrations copyright © 1999 by Rosalind Beardshaw
Printed in Hong Kong. All rights reserved.
Library of Congress catalog card number: 99-71630
ISBN 0-06-028621-0
First American edition, 2000
http://www.harperchildrens.com

Fran's Flower

by Lisa Bruce   illustrated by Rosalind Beardshaw

■ HarperCollinsPublishers

One day Fran found a flowerpot filled with soil.
Poking out of the top was a tiny green tip.
"I will grow this flower," Fran said to Fred.

She took it home.
"Grow flower," she said.
But the tip stayed tiny.

"I think this flower is hungry," Fran said.

So Fran went to the fridge.
Inside she found some of her favorite food.

She gave the flower a slice of pizza.

The next day Fran gave it a piece of cheeseburger.

Then she gave it spaghetti, two chocolate chip cookies and a large spoonful of strawberry ice cream.

She even gave it one of Fred's juicy bones.

But the flower didn't grow. The tip stayed tiny.
Fran got fed up.

"Silly flower!" Fran said, and she threw it out the back door.

The flowerpot fell onto the ground and rolled away. The rain fell on it.

The wind blew on it.

The sun shone on it.

Finally, the tiny green tip grew . . .

and grew . . .

and grew.

Until one day Fran and
Fred went outside to play.

When they opened the door, a surprise was waiting . . .

A big beautiful flower—just for Fran!

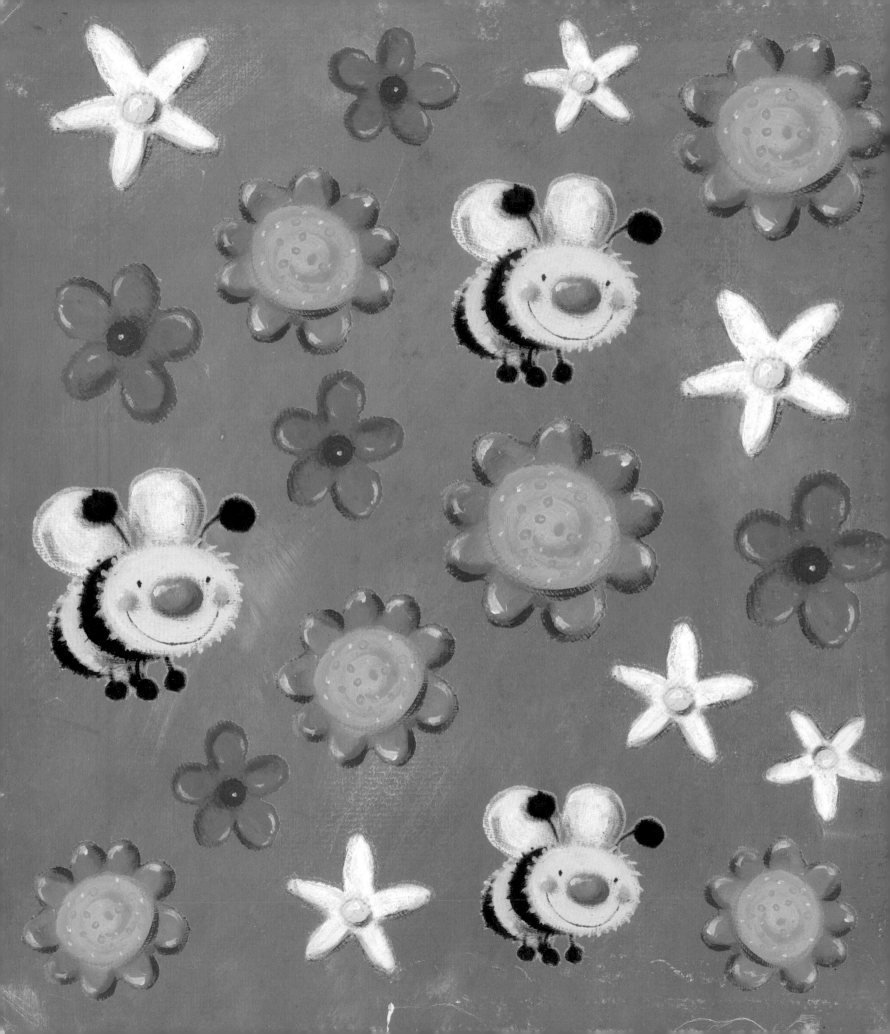